Kiss me deadly

Baciami mortalmente

As seen through a young man's eyes

Published by Ricky Dale

Publishing partner: Paragon Publishing, Rothersthorpe

First published 2024

© Ricky Dale 2024

The rights of Ricky Dale to be identified as the author of this work have been asserted by him in accordance with the Copyright, Designs and Patents Act of 1988.

All rights reserved; no part of this publication may be reproduced, stored in a retrieval system, or transmitted in any form or by any means, electronic, mechanical, photocopying, recording or otherwise without the prior written consent of the publisher or a licence permitting copying in the UK issued by the Copyright Licensing Agency Ltd. www.cla.co.uk

ISBN 978-1-78792-069-9

Book design, layout and production management by Into Print
www.intoprint.net
+44 (0)1604 832149

Acknowledgements

In order to make any novel an impressive achievement, one needs to be surrounded by a host of good friends and professionals who have that certain 'know-how'.

My good fortune is to have amassed such a group, without whom my novels would struggle to fruition.

A to Z they are as follows:
    Action Stationers – Peter Layland
    Montreal Editing - Dianne Letky
    PC Doctor - Jon Manley
    Social Media Co. – Christelle Louise Shuttleworth
    Torquay Photo Centre – Ras Virdee

Special thanks indeed to Paragon Publishing and Mark and Anne Webb for agreeing to publish this novel – moreover, for all the other novels they have published for me.

And of course, my beloved daughter: Dr. Kimberley Jayne.

How the story finally emerged on paper!

I'd been intending to write *Kiss Me Deadly* for gazillions of decades, but sadly lacked the courage of my own convictions.Fundamentally, the gist of the story is relating to a dab portion of my adolescence which I choose to disregard.

Nevertheless, it was during the autumn of 2023 that the story began to cross my mind again. To be quite frank my seventh novel *Siobhan's Bitches* had only recently been published and I was seeking some new and empirical ideas!

However, before I was able to give 'KMD' a respectable shot, I became unwell for several months and as a result the whole darn shebang was assigned to the back burner once again.

Now it seems to me that when one is indisposed, the ominous choice becomes 'push-up daisies', or 'mend'. Fortunately, in RD's situation he was able to plump for the latter!

From day one, to bring the story to a conclusion on or before December 2024 is the thing I had to be sure of. For me and me alone, it was my crucial prerequisite. Thankfully, by early spring 2024, I felt well enough to buckle down to my writing and to

Ricky Dale's

burn the midnight oil if necessary.

So there you have it; on schedule and in style. A remembrance that Candelaria* would have intended; and what's more, she would have been proud of yours truly for fixing it all up!

Ricky Dale

Candelaria Dale, 1946 to 1964

Prologue

"An Ontario summer is like a woman. Ripe, hotly passionate and oftentimes playfully capricious."

With these words I begin my current novel *Kiss Me Deadly*.

Over the years letters have arrived from a variety of readers as a rejoiner to my previous novels. Many with kind thoughts and good wishes. But moreover, a fair percentage wanted to know what had first encouraged me to write *Kiss Me Deadly*.

For reasons not entirely clear to me, the prompt to write it had crossed my mind on numerous occasions. However, it always seemed to finish up on the back-burner – possibly because I didn't have the courage!

In any event, and for the curious folk among you, I finally made up my mind to roll off an openly unfeigned life's chronological spanning my younger years. An aperçu, if you like, of both the great and the not so great!

I think it's important to point out – and not at all for the literary licence – a tweak here and there that I was obliged to make!

I did, on occasion, find that it was 'de rigueur' to adjust or make changes to some, but not all, of the more revealing aspects of the story. The last thing that I wanted was for the narrative to become a 'testimony' of sorts.

In particular, sensitive Cosa Nostra incidents – which cannot be authenticated in any event – have been deliberately precluded from the novel and, indeed, the original manuscripts too.

For me personally, KMD is a book of endings and new beginnings and, in between, are my own boyhood wonderings; for what they are worth!

Be that as it may, the book per se attempts to encapsulate in a few words the enigmatical 'Candelaria'! Her steadfastness; the way she could talk around the clock; the fragrance of her freshly washed hair.

From the onset of writing this prologue I knew I had to overcome that tendency I have to keep alluding to her – honestly, I couldn't.

Kiss Me Deadly

Leading Persons

'Mom'	Mother of Lynn and Ricky
Lynn and Ricky	Twin sister and brother
Canderlaria (Sherry)	Daughter of Rocco Zito
Rocco Zito	Mafioso 'Boss'
Edward G	Mafioso 'Inquisitor'
Elroy	Entrepreneur – and Mom's fancy man
Guy Lombardo	Maestro
Jayne Mansfield	Entertainer

'Also ran'

George	The chicken farmer
Chico Fernandez	Percussionist
Mad Dan	'Other worldly' bootlegger

One

An Ontario summer is like a woman. Ripe, hotly passionate and oftentimes playfully capricious. She comes quickly and goes as she pleases, although one is never sure whether she will come at all, or for that matter, how long she will stay.

Despite this, the story about my women is disapprovingly brief. Yet still like an Ontario summer she was able to spread herself over the countryside and make everything hurtfully beautiful to the eye.

Almost everything that I wanted to write about her, I tried and failed. On account of a bizarre occurrence cutting in whenever I put pen to paper. It's as though my script had already been written for me, but upon blank pages! In fact, my new role is no longer that of a storyteller per se. Conversely it has become similar in nature to that of a meticulous archaeologist! How so? Inasmuch that all I have to do is simply peel away the non-transparent matter in order to provide visibility and understanding for all concerned.

Ricky Dale's

The notion being that Ricky Dale as author of this storyline is, in effect, merely the bearer of a confused message between two very different worlds. Rather like a go-between in a strange seemingly endless conundrum of so-called fate and circumstance.

Backward looking, I prefer to imagine that the storyline that forms this melee is fictional. That way I don't have to deal with a misdirected nauseous world of another individual whose seediness aggressively encroached within the bounds of our world; the distillation of events I have chosen to forget,

Conceivably so, I have wanted to contribute some sort of written testimony in order to help rebuff one or some negative aspects of those injurious days. Perhaps bring to the fore, instead, much of the positivity and humorous tittle-tattle that at times dominated and simplistically enriched our lives. Those innocent infatuations so endlessly endearing from the perspective of one and all. Moreover, it has become essential, of late, to at last find a desirable spot in the annals of time-worn memories, where misunderstanding and wickedness can evaporate in their entirety.

Even at this late date, I cannot hand on heart swear that oftentimes, in some irrelevant way, I had been complicit to various notorious slayings. I wasn't an accomplice or anything of that nature, but I do fess up to being there at the time.

Sometimes it was a territorial dispute or maybe an inter-family deal that went wrong. But, whatever the reason, it was an indication to me of how certain members of Cosa Nostra were prepared to go. At one stage I was lodging at the Brant. One evening the red carpet was put out because of a visit by big Mafia boss 'Joe Bananas'. At seventeen years of age, I thought his name was really cool!

My boss was an old-style 'brokester' who was appreciative that I knew how to keep my mouth shut and seriously knew my place, and he enjoyed my singing too! It never crossed my mind that I may need to be silenced, it just wasn't an issue. The Niagara Escarpment was though – for that reason I kept less than gabby!

Silence, remoteness, wisdom, power: these are watchwords that govern the behaviour of the senior ranks of Cosa Nostra.

Two

Our dad was a Canadian national who, during WW2, was stationed in the South Hams area of South Devon, England. Mom was a local girl from Harburtonford but lived on base with Dad and the other couples – they were referred to as 'camp wives'.

One winter evening when Mom was pregnant with my sister Lynn and me, her water broke halfway through the movie 'Holy Matrimony'. It starred the British actress Gracie Fields – the girl with the heavy English accent – especially when she sang 'White Cliffs of Dover'.

Mom told us that her and Dad were sitting in the middle of the last row in the balcony of the crowded Empire Picture House in Kingsbridge, Devon. They were so close to the glittering ceiling lights, Mom said she felt she was 'up with the stars'.

Apparently, Lynn and me took 24 hours to arrive. Mom commented that she was certain she was going to die – said that none of those old wives passed on that it hurt to bear children!

Lynn and I still don't know, to this day, which of us was the first to arrive – although I oftentimes refer to her as my 'baby sister'.

Dad was an infantry serviceman; Mom told us he was the very best of the sharpshooters in his unit. He had been a dreamer and had fantasized about joining the cavalry and chasing the Nazis across Europe on a horse! Mom recounted how the second world war would oftentimes become a Sunday dinner table allegory with sugar-coated symbolic meanings. She said it helped him make some sense out of what he was being expected to do. Like so many of his compatriots, our Dad failed to return from the beaches at Normandy – June 6, 1944.

On many numerous occasions Lynn and I would fall asleep on Mom's lap just listening to her purr through 'White Cliffs of Dover', over again.

Three

Genetically transmitted information of a biased and misleading nature has been used ad infinitum to promote and convince by some-such political regime or executive; and mostly they pull it off! One day folks may get wise that it's purely disseminated propaganda for the masses and nothing more.

The hapless and wretched truth is that after WW2 seemingly 'chipper' old England was not a bit joyous and light-hearted as the hype told us we were! Factually our country was little more than an exhausted flea-bitten mutt. Without any moral principles of right or wrong, our poor knackered country was running amok with no sense of direction.

Food rationing queues continued well into the 1950s. The majority of children were abashed by rickets or such and those English faces were all angles and bones at best. Even coal and coke were rationed!

The fearsome Sword of Damocles hanging over us all was the Bomb; however, that was the least of our worries!

Four

Dear old England was a shambles the day we all travelled to London to Canada House. Our migration status was quickly cut and dried, being as our Dad was a Canadian citizen. Lynn and I were just whippersnappers at the time; however, we were old enough to join a line of revellers at a street party celebration – it didn't mean much to us at the time but Mom said Churchill had been returned to power (dismissed by electorate in 1945).

August was on the brink of September and although summer was melting away fast, us kids, nevertheless, thoroughly made whoopee once we were at last shipboard.

The swimming pool seemed so adventurous an experience and the everyday newsreels were always followed by oodles of cartoons. They had what we were told was a 'buffet', it was a kind of cafeteria where passengers can help themselves – repeatedly if they wish! For the most part we stuffed our bellies with ice cream and cake – unheard of sumptuousness in Harburtonford!

We later found out that our lovely Mom had been enjoying her own whoopee too – with this really neat ship's officer! Supposedly he was out of order; fraternising with a passenger; but be that as it may our Mom was blessed with a profound charm and audacious recklessness as well!

Mom viewed our migration to Dad's country of origin with a kind of courteous detachment. She didn't necessarily have a huge penchant for Canada; however, Canada was on offer without any lengthy and complicated rigmarole. She applauded that kind of approbation that her and her family were indeed 'sought-after'; it appealed to the neediness she was desperate for, after the loss of her husband.

I have oftentimes speculated on how our lives would have worked out had Australia been our country of choice. Puts me in mind of a Canadian saying that I picked up years later: *'Yeah, and if my aunt had nuts, she'd be my uncle'*!

Five

It had taken us approaching seven days to journey from Southampton to Montreal. I think it's benevolent of Lynn when she insists on referring to Montreal as 'The New World'. Mom, on the other hand, had us hot footing all over the place until we'd found a Greyhound bound for Toronto, which she insists on referring to as 'English Territory'.

We put-up in Toronto for several days, checking out the local blurbs and visiting realtors. Finally, we hit on a Charles Harris, a deferential realtor situated on Eglington Avenue East. There was no doubt in my mind that this tiny stooped gentleman was indubitably going to be the fundamental curve to reshape our future.

Mom figures – and rightly so – that a commercial property would be beneficial inasmuch that we would have a roof over our heads and a means to earn a living too. With that in mind we chanced on this property out on the highway #20 and Charles had been in favour of it too!

Ricky Dale's

'Winter Creek Country Inn' had been unoccupied for several years. Although it looked somewhat neglected it surely had positive potential. Price tag: It had been waiting so patiently for a Mom and her two kids! The forecourt was a large open area with three enormous chinaberry trees about midway. We all agreed that it was patently obvious that the trees sold it to us!

Six

Our nearest neighbour was 'The Golden Gloves' motel which was roughly around two miles north of Winter Creek Inn. In the other direction was the relatively smallish community of Jonesville – 930 population. Although The Golden Gloves and Jonesville were potential neighbours, folks in the village snubbed the motel with a vengeance. There is truly a logical justification for this stand-off attitude, which I intend to shed light upon in future chapters.

It was early in the am when my sleep was interrupted by a loud shrill of voices coming from downstairs. Mom and Lynn had made a discovery and were almost beside themselves in excitement. Our family had had so very many 'hullabaloos' of late that I honestly believe we would feel somewhat neglected if our lives were to move forward in a conventional manner. However, almost jumping into my bathrobe I flew down those stairs really quick! By all accounts, Mom and Lynn had been doing an early morning exploration of the restaurants higgledy-piggledy layout, and had decided to break open the ancient snap-lock on the unutilised door of the basement. Not waiting for me, they had instead ventured down the rickety wooden staircase to the basement proper and were giving the whole cadaverous lower ground floor an obsessive once-over!

Peeping through the darkness toward the far end of the basement Mom shrieked 'it's an old fogeyish "still", used for distilling alcoholic drinks such as whisky'. Lynn was beginning to get a real buzz from all the unexpected excitement: 'boot-leggers and Gatsby' – our new home is synonymous with full-scale gangsters and racketeers. She loved every minute of it!

By and by, our customers enlightened us as to the history of Winter Creek Inn and, in particular, our basement. A folk tale most probably, however I am inclined to believe it!

Apparently (so the story goes) our basement was the home of a doolally character whom the locals had nicknamed 'Mad Dan'. During the prohibition era he was the so-called 'wine-maker'.

Although the sale of bootleg booze and such was outlawed, transporting the illegal alcohol across the border and into the United States was big business. Dan was reported to have said 'A man has a right to make whisky as long as he makes it on his own land'. However, one night, he was firing up the still for another batch of booze when interstate revenue men burst in. During the forthcoming incursion the still overheated and spat hot ethyl into his face. Dan had completely disappeared before the revenue men were able to respond.

Many believed that, having doused himself in Winter Creek, he attempted to cross over to the other side but drowned. It's also rumoured that he hides out in the thick undergrowth that encompasses the creek, unaware that the prohibition era is over. It's told that spasmodically he returns to his basement home for solace.

Lynn really bought into the supernatural and hereafter big time. She didn't pooh-pooh the suggestion of Mad Dan's earthly or indeed spiritual presence, no matter how preposterous it may sound to others.

Be that as it may, her serious side kicked in when she added: 'If he's not already conked out, he will be – happen he tangles with me'. There was a touch of bitterness in her voice too!

Over the great bridge, with the sunlight though the girders making a constant flicker upon the moving cars, with the city rising up across the river in white heaps and sugar lumps all built with a wish out of non-olfactory money.

Ricky Dale's

The city seen from the Queensboro Bridge is always the city seen for the first time, in its first wild promise of all the mystery and beauty in the world.

From: The Great Gatsby (F. Scott Fitzgerald, 1925)

Seven

It didn't take Mom and us kids long before we'd cleansed and cleaned out that scabby old basement. Never before was Winter Creek Inn scrubbed and spotless in its entirety. With my limited knowledge of carpentry, I even managed to construct a modest chicken coop to the rear of the restaurant.

The idea began when our charming Greek neighbour George Papadopalos presented us with a dozen Rhode Island Reds. George was proprietor of an immensely populated chicken farm just along highway #20. Dear George was Methuselah personified, but a more courteous person you couldn't wish to meet. He would partake of two coffees every morning at precisely 10.30am. Always neatly attired in his frayed three-piece suit and worse for wear necktie – knotted tight around a skinny neck. He oftentimes would blurt out to me in his fractured English, that I was lucky to have such a 'spunky' Mom and sister. He was the spunky one – perhaps this great and unique region goads folks into becoming spunky, eh?

Lynn once insightfully observed that our new venture was purely a 'horse and buggy' prelude to what's going to be awaiting our family up ahead. 'Compared to England, this country is an achiever's paradise if you allow it to be' she added.

Mom was always given to using modest or even godly type sentences. I recall her interceding Lynn's remark by adding: 'It's mainly due to our family having more religious devotion to inevitable events'. I pondered over what she had meant, that night just before I went to sleep. All in all, I arrived at the same conclusion as she did!

Turning Point

The road turns here,
Up ahead you can see it
Dissolving in the dust
Dissolving into me
Telling me
Hang on
But
Let go.

Ricky Dale's

Eight

Invariably it takes a period of time to become integrated and wholeheartedly accepted in small town Ontario. Mom, Lynn and yours truly had managed to accomplish that humble miracle with acclaim. Oftentimes segment by segment but got there in the end!

The apathetic De Roche family who had previously owned the business, allowed it to go to rack and ruin. And when it fell into total disrepair they packed up and hightailed back to Montreal. In my opinion the village folk were seemingly more slanted toward us because of the English connection – the collision of French and British interests had been a threatening conflict in North America since the 1700s!!

I am also pleased to report that our Winter Creek Inn has damn quick become the adopted 'headquarters' of our Jonesville baseball and hockey teams and that, furthermore, we are headlined on the front cover of the local entertainments programme too!

Mom wisely enlightened us kids by her mention

that the most valuable aspect of winning over the local hucksters, is to show them your veneration of respect and interest in their sporting preoccupations! For example: Japan has its sumo wrestling; the UK has its association football.

Ricky Dale's

Sundays

Sundays are a joy
On the playing field
When the players dress
So smart!

Please God grant me absolution
For the other days
Which I waste.
But let me waste

Some
Several dozen
Sundays
More!

Nine

It seems now to have become something of a tradition at Winter Creek Inn that Saturday evenings are reserved mainly for the town senior citizens and local business folk. Mom had that gathering covered too!

She figured on making a huge contribution to her more sophisticated clientele understanding exactly what type or method of cooking suits them the best.

This particular Saturday evening she planned on educating folk on the versatility of desserts. Perhaps even to include country or region as well.

Right toward the end of the extremely enlightening 'seminar' about desserts, the thing that tickled me was Mom's amusing banter on deep frying, as follows:

'Put any folks near any piece of nicely cooked food and they are sure to want it flung into a deep fryer – or cover it with sugar – or flung into a deep fryer and then cover it with sugar.' (*Admit it; you could just go for something deep-fried and sugar-coated right about*

Ricky Dale's

now, couldn't you?)[1]

---

1   This is precisely why 'Tim Hortons' – aka Coffee Time, represents the apex of mature Canadian cuisine.

Everything in a Tim Hortons – including the counter-tops (completely), the staff (inevitably), and the customers (eventually), are covered with a fine layer of warm grease and dusted with icing sugar!

It seems to me that us more mature and somewhat (sometimes) more influential Canadians are absolutely poles apart from their opposite numbers in the good old UK. Unfortunately, they haven't got around to inviting deep fryers into their country yet! 'Unpardonable' says Mom.

Ten

The pure exuberance of a cool early morning, here at The Winter Creek Inn, nestling like an aged songbird that still recollects the tune but is too lazy to leave its nest. Highway #20, no longer the bustling rural route to Niagara, no longer the coloured storyboard of a thousandfold vacationists. Moreso like an historical figure bathed with the mosaic prayers of yesteryear's pre-eminence. On the highway the fallen leaves make such a gay crackling noise when the bushed tyres of some multi-truck crushed them disapprovingly.

Working in the restaurant/dairy bar in the early am, there was always a variety of questions to settle, before the day proper gets underway. Ponderous, cumbersome questions, and like a scholar, I was becoming simply exhausted just attempting to connect the dots!

It takes a mighty strong-minded individual to make one's mind up when there are so, so many alternatives and substitutes available: 20 types of

Ricky Dale's

breakfast cereal with 6 types of thick velvety cream. A dozen different bakes of ring donuts with various sprinkles. Crisp bacon with eggs over lightly, button mushrooms and fried tomatoes, pancakes, waffles, maple syrup – the list is endless!

I enjoyed playing the Wurlitzer in the early mornings too. In any event I was able to choose what records I liked. Not so to the raggamuffin radiogram of late. On whatever occasion I switch it on I hear the whinging strains of 'I want to hold your hand' or some such unpleasant racket! Where are those illustrious and greatly loved musicians and performers who have been defending their very souls from the slippery God-awful British invaders of late? Gene Vincent, Chuck Berry, Elvis – where are you, my friends?

I've never been a black or white fly on the wall, however of late my mind has been preoccupied to the disturbing lack of justice that we all are palmed off with from time to time. For example: just several months ago the genius bandleader Cab Calloway had been given a 'back seat' to the status seeking Beatles, during a recent Ed Sullivan show. Calloway was a real pro by comparison to the so-called 'fab four'. I guess it was down to those jittering hyperventilating girls that swayed Ed's decision, eh?!

Kiss Me Deadly

I guess we are all falling
We never learn about it
Until we land.
Paul might indeed have fallen
A different way
But who's to say which
Way is better
Until they've been there –
And come back safe?

Ricky Dale's

Eleven

A dark blue saloon pulled up outside the restaurant. Lifting the powdered dust on Winter Creek's unfinished forecourt. The stone-faced driver put me in mind of the Edward G. Robinson character, the pugnacious hoodlum in the 1930's movie 'Little Caesar'.

Don't you find it uncanny how oftentimes we jump to a conclusion when seeing and summing up a person for the very first time? Be that as it may, this guy had the expressive intensity of an old guard moonshiner – looked as though he'd kill without hesitation any unfortunate who, through their own wilfulness, didn't entirely grasp his rules.

The passenger in the rear of the Chevy, I hadn't noticed immediately due to my preoccupation with the 'chauffeur'. But now, as I poured my second cup of Chase & Sanborn, how was I to know that this significant moment in time is one I should savour. This precise inordinate moment a protected secret world would take hold of everything I knew or was about to know!

The young woman passenger looked to me as though she arrived to preach the second coming of Christ, however (jumping to conclusion again), I'd remembered that Mom had mentioned she's hired a 'everyday girl, to help out', and this obviously was our new waitress.

As she stepped from the vehicle the first sight of her gave me an awareness that was difficult to comprehend at first. Prompted me to make some fresh coffee anyway, strong and black!

It seems to me that from time to time, it's not unusual for a person to be taken completely unawares – knowingly caught off-guard as it were. For some apparent reason that's the spot I found myself in, right now!

Although she walked toward me with a stylish demeanour, her clothes kind of betrayed her. They really looked as though she had been the sole survivor of a closet purge that hadn't gone according to plan! Allow me to elucidate for you: She wore an embroidered peasant blouse, together with an exceptionally full skirt gathered at the waist and decorated by sequins. A stole loosely over her shoulders was also decorated by sequins. She clutched a kind of gold lamé purse – stolen from Theda Bara, no doubt! Not even a gob of lipstick or mascara and tits fatuously false or genuine? Guesswork at best!

But hell – just because her appearance per se contradicted the norm, what does it really matter, just as long as she is proficient at waiting tables, eh?

Our apartment above Winter Creek Inn was abundantly generous. It was spread over two floors and inwardly it felt more like a regular house than an apartment. High windows, fireplace in the bedrooms and a wide staircase leading to the bedrooms.

'*RICKY!*' Mom hollers from the bathroom, 'is that our little girl with the braces?'

'Yes, it's the new waitressing girl Mom' I retorted mockingly.

'Then I'm going to have an extra half an hour in bed!' says Mom.

Twelve

It seemed to me that a dime in the Wurlitzer might be perfect as an ice-breaker! 'D'ya like Ronnie Hawkins and The Hawks?' I enquired instinctively. She was sat on a swivel stool at the kitchen end of the dairy bar, and her face lit-up at my question. 'Yes, I do like Ronnie, but I prefer Frankie Valli' she smilingly replied. The time-worn jukebox began slowly making its selection of goodies. 'Why d'ya like him?' I pressed. 'Because his relatives all originate from Castelluccio, same as my Dad' she replied. I looked at her slightly puzzled. 'It's a remote area in central Italy' she briskly added. As if on cue, the rhythm section cut in followed by Frankie's frenetic vocals! 'My brother took me to see him – it was a bitterly cold evening and he was playing to a sparse crowd – mostly fans – on the shore of Lake Simcoe. I've been a follower of Frankie's ever since then' she smiled quite smugly.

I decided upon giving her one of my curious far-reaching explanatories: 'Have you ever considered

Ricky Dale's

that your Frankie might indeed have the hots for you? And in that regard his Sherry song might be specifically aimed at how it would feel being on a date with you?' She kind of hooted dispassionately 'is that an Englishman's empty-headed observation – please do explain!' 'Listen to me' I replied very openly; 'us English guys know all that there is about dating a girl – and it differs considerably from actually being on a date per se. Inasmuch that if you were to win over the baby boy's Italian momma, being on the actual date is a cinch!' Se eyed me up sadly; 'I'm not so sure that I agree with you. For example, my birth name is Candelaria, so my name is not going to complement their Frankie's song!' I gave her a cheeky, knowing look; 'I am going to miss you Candelaria, not in a negative way though.' Swallowing hard I continued 'from now onwards you will be known as Sherry!'

Thirteen

Highway #20; an undisturbed backwoods as highways go, and the gateway to Hamilton, Toronto and Niagara Falls too. Golden Gloves Motel was also situated of Highway #20 and it also had an important connection with the aforementioned cities.

Golden Gloves Motel was additionally Sherry's family home inasmuch that the family was forcefully obliged to abandon their home in Italy and relocate to Canada. The motel had, of late, become a home-from-home administrative centre of the Organisation and satisfied the needs of many French and Canadian mobsters out of Marseilles. It did indeed have its own Mafia family who, in those days, were led by Vincent Cotroni who, in turn, was allied to the Bonanno family in New York.

With regard to Sherry's father Rocco Zito; he had worked as a boxer and a stuntman after prohibition had become less fashionable. In recent times he had risen to becoming the highest-ranking ascendancy to the syndicate in that region of Southern Ontario.

Although Montreal, Toronto and New York had always been the main staging posts, Sherry's father was located nicely in between those principal cities and, as main 'organiser', he gave a precise meaning to what had become know as 'Rocco's European Tours'. This involved a steady flow of holidaying Italian and French families, traveling by liner to Montreal – along with cars specially fitted out. When they'd travelled on to see the sights of New York (naturally enough) the cars would, of course, be relieved of their hidden burdens!

I recall watching the TV one evening in what we at Winter Creek Inn had named 'The Banquet Room'. It was simply a large room attached to the main restaurant. But what made it unique was the oak wooden panel walls and the high-level hidden lighting. The room was reserved for our VIP guests only. Among others that evening we were playing host to the notorious 'no-nonsense' mafioso heavy Joe Valachi! I found the whole experience that evening kind of surreal to say the least: here I was playing host to a gangster who simultaneously was on my TV screen!

Joe Valachi was a syndicate soldier who, it was claimed, was ordered by Rocco Zito (Sherry's father) to undertake a killing.

The New York Commission was finally set up to ascertain what exactly occurred and who was responsible. To cut a long story short Valachi from the onset didn't intend to give the New York Commission any latitude at all, indeed he pipped them at the post with every unpleasant aspersion they threatened him with. Valachi was one of a vanishingly rare species who had learned long ago how to play both sides against one another. He revealed categorically that no Capi would ever be so contentious to have had any direct or indirect involvement in any crime of that nature. Eventually the Commission's defence was declared null and void and Valachi was acquitted.[2]

---

2   Organised crime is perhaps the most infamous phenomenon of our time. From Al Capone, who boldly claimed his bootlegging activities were a public service, to the flamboyant Teflon Don, John Gotti. Their crimes, scheme, hangouts and unique culture are oftentimes something to behold; and other times will fill you with fear and apprehensiveness!

Ricky Dale's

Fourteen

Our Sherry and yours truly had developed an efficient and organised system for dealing and coping with the extremely high influx of summer customers, particularly the American tourists.

We didn't want any of our guests to be so inclined as to bitch, and sit there with arms crossed, because our service didn't live up to expectations. Nippy, zippy, that was us, and the rewards (tips!) were generous. Winter Creek Inn was situated only a score or so miles from the United States border crossing, and during July and August I solemnly swear that the entire populations of Buffalo and Michigan were either savouring Mom's cow pie or splashing around with the snappers in Winter Creek.

Mom, Lynn and I were on seriously good terms with our local baseball team, in fact they tended to use Winter Creek Inn as their 'dug out'.[3] On more

---

[3] An area where players sit when they are not actively engaged on the pitch.

than one occasion the team had pitched in to wash dishes and clear tables upon realising how pushed we were.

Having said that, and as we were relatively 'new' Canadians, we were nevertheless still finding our feet with regard to Canadian culture per se.

One of the aspects of the local demeanour that we were finding difficult to absorb was the disapproving attitude some locals had toward our Sherry. They tended to treat her as though she was some kind of panhandler; when in fact she was a local girl from a local family.

There seemed to us no good reason why folks chose to not only ignore Sherry but, at the same time, to treat her with such a grim non-courteous detachment. Almost as though this slight slip of a girl was endowed with some kind of tyrannical presence!

Our nit-picking ingenuousness from across the pond was credible only by its pure cockeyed stupidity. Inasmuch as we hadn't chanced upon Cosa Nostra in 1950s blighty, as yet!

The young guys, in and around the same age as our Sherry did, however, have a good repartee with all our other waitresses though. Mostly pure chaff of course! Take Cathy for instance. Cathy was an 'attractively plump' large bosomy girl who, to her discredit, insisted upon wearing outrageously short cut skirts. Also, to her discredit (from this writer's standpoint) was that she had become a huge fan of the Beatles of late!

The news spread when Cathy came to work for us and pretty soon our local guys became heavy hitting smokers. Inasmuch that all of the more popular brands of smokes were kept on the top shelves – which necessitated our Cathy standing on a chair in order to reach same!

It seems to me that Whitie our baseball team captain was the scallywag who totally described Cathy's 'high' jinks as 'she's a fine drawn-out lady – never did have a taste for those wimmin whose cheekbones stick out'. I recall someone adding 'for Christ's sake, who the hell looks at her cheekbones anyway'!

Mom's realistic response was that her boys (she referred to them as 'her boys') 'seldom care a damn about other things in a woman besides their tits and ass!' Mom was always (invariably) right regarding these matters, because when Cathy wasn't on duty their conversation consisted of nothing more than hot dogs, football and latest episode of Bonanza!

Kiss Me Deadly

Fifteen

Sherry and yours truly spent her school vacation running rings around the floor of Winter Creek's restaurant and dairy bar. We worked well together and to our credit we heaped up oodles of tips. Time just flew by, especially during the late afternoons and early evenings when Sherry's shifts ended. The formidable anticipation of Sherry's 'chauffeur' arriving to ferry her home was ever present in my mind.

We kind of touched one another with a slushy unspoken besottedness. Once in a while I wondered what was on her mind. We had a curiously discombobulated relationship, if indeed a 'relationship' was the accurate illustrative of what we did have. It's honest-to-goodness that I did want a little more but pondered on whether she did too. Of late she had begun to give me a diminutive kiss either on the cheek or mouth; when it was time for her to leave. Is this the beginning of what dreams are made of, or is it entirely my make-believe assumption and just momentary madness?

Ricky Dale's

I want to say I love you,
Yet, I'm afraid that if I do,
You'll laugh, and call me silly.
Or maybe I'm afraid that you'll
Be afraid too
And end it all
Before it begins.

There are times
When I wish that I
Could read your mind
But then again there
Are other moments
When I'm so glad
That I can't;
Especially those times
When your thoughts
Don't include me
And what could be.

Sixteen

Winter Creek Country Inn per se, had sprung up in the latter part of the 19th century. It had been a hostelry or beer parlour but turned its attention to being and eatery after WW2.

I have oftentimes speculated upon where the creek begins its journey and where it ends. I would imagine it begins in or around Hamilton, Ontario, and ends into the great Niagara River.

For me and our English family Winter Creek was a mythological place to us. During the tremendously scorching summer months the grass and vegetation on the banks of the creek is sparse and thinly scattered; however, during each spring and fall the whole area becomes a miraculous sight to behold. Snapping turtles home in the cooler parts of the creek and wide-branched trees litter the banks in abundance – their leafy tops dusty green and cicada filled, just waiting for rain. The winter arrives specifically to allow us to skate, toboggan and to create snowmen! And we reign supreme over each and every aspect of its lyrical richness.

Seventeen

It was usually just before 2:30pm that Sherry and yours truly would hang up our waiting apparel, don an apron and get to grips with our potato peeling chores. The by far most significant roles as a restauranteur is related to potato peeling. French fries (chips!) are indeed the mainstay of which virtually everything else on the menu depends, and also the predominant making of every illustrious nosh-up – no matter what side of the pond you hail from!

Peeling and falling in love are a perfect combination to scurry the afternoon away, until Mom's dulcet voice calling from the restaurant, telling us 'that's enough for today kids'. Not unlike two little Okies from Muskogee we scrubbed up fairly well, and in a jiffy were spruced up in our waiting attire again and ready for the evening influx of customers.

Our Mom could be bordering on schoolmarmish with regard to the way in which her workforce behaved and indeed their appearance – family or otherwise she didn't differentiate between the two.

Oftentimes it was even money as to whether our uniforms were starched or not. On this particular occasion we had run low on starch, on account of us using it up on the soaked potatoes.

Mom put across her argument by pointing out that there were many exacting folk who still do appreciate a touch of etiquette and stylishness, even out here in the boondocks!

A typical case lesson was that very evening, when just before it became dimsickle, a classy elegant husband and wife seated themselves by the fireplace opposite the large plate glass mirror – which was faraway from the other clientele. I noticed that they had been easing their eyes on Lynn and me and obviously liked us and the fact that we were attentive toward them. Later on, in the evening when the restaurant had become more subdued, the lady beckoned Lynn and me to join them at their table.

Apparently, the couple were proprietors of the chic Pines Hotel at Stony Creek – a renowned and extremely celebrated establishment just outside of Hamilton, Ontario.

Having introduced themselves the gentleman seemed committed to finding out whether we would consider employment at the Pines Hotel: 'a more desirable post, to which you both be better suited' he seriously indicated. I felt somewhat taken aback by the impression we had made and I could see that our Lynn felt the same. For a moment we hesitated; giving the gentleman time to lean back comfortably in his chair. 'They really don't know', he addressed his wife. I shook my head and replied 'know what?' The lady looked me straight in the eye in disbelief and began a preamble that even to this day it touches me: 'It's so uncommon to come across an extraordinary couple such as yourselves who have an almost superhuman attachment and unique rapport between one another, that it is communicated in an existential way to their patrons – this remarkable bond is normally only found in twins.' And then jestfully she added 'you're not twins. Are you?'

Almost as if on cue, Mom poked her head around the scullery partition: 'hope my kids are not rankling you too much, we rarely are privileged by guests such as you fine folk – the previous being Premier Diefenbaker's visit in 1957!' I turned to face Mom with the best supercilious smile on my face that I could muster: 'sorry Mom, it's with regret that Lynn and I are going to offer you our notice that we are leaving. You see we have been afforded a more lucrative placement at the ritzy Pines in Stony Creek forthwith.'

I had seldom seen or indeed imagined such a high-class lady become so tongue-tied, embarrassed and red-faced, and a gentleman apologising so profusely. However, so as not to allow matters to escalate, Mom quickly took control of the situation with a loud burst of laughter: 'hey dear folks, you are welcome to both of them – been trying to rid myself of that son and daughter of mine for years; my daughter likes her own reflection, and my son has become love-lopped by a Sicilian mobster's daughter, so you take 'em both!' Mom removed her pinny and the five of us sat around the restaurant bar chuckling and chortling about who wants our kids, and our immunity to Canadian Club malt whisky!

'Why is it that the question we often discern, is the question we often pursue?'

Marcel Proust

Ricky Dale's

Eighteen

It seems to me that there are several pivotal points in life where you could easily fall down Alice's rabbit hole and find that life has significantly changed for you. Suddenly, right there and then, you begin to become a different entity than you imagined you were before.

The heavy snowfall had muffled my world into a simple stillness. Large unwieldy flakes fell without an utterance – the wind also was hushed beyond comprehension. A voice from my radio seemed to have swept through every nook and cranny of Winter Creek Inn, astonishing my ears and breaking my soul. The news was too overwhelming, it rendered me powerless. Watching the snow fall in profusion through the cold plate glass windows will, for me, always be so associated with his death – inked in whiteness of that God awful day!

'Three of the world's top rock 'n' roll singing stars: Richie Valens, JP The Big Bopper Richardson, and

Buddy Holly, died in a crash of a chartered plane today.'

I breathed deeply, lifted my heavy hands and covered my face and attempted to think of something else – anything else would suffice; apart from that fateful winter morning in 1959!

*'Just you know why
Why you and I
Will by and by
Know true love ways'*

Ricky Dale's

Nineteen

Elroy was a regular at Winter Creek Inn, we'd oftentimes yarn away, and before long we became pals. In due course he'd additionally become our Mom's fancy man. Description: I guess that Elroy was something of a wheeler-dealer. Back in England we'd offhand refer to flashily dressed guys like Elroy as 'spivs'.

From time to time, during the early evenings, I'd taken to crooning away a few popular ballads for the more appreciative clientele. Lynn (if she felt so inclined) would every so often accompany me on an out of the ark pianoforte, we'd discovered at the Trading Post. All of this drew Elroy's attention, but the seeds were really sown when he persuaded Sherry to duet with me. Although our rehearsal was a token minimal, nevertheless it all worked out well.

On the Saturday evening when we all debuted proper, Elroy introduced us as 'the breeziest package this side of Niagara Falls'. Lynn and I liked Elroy a lot. The fact that he was 'doing' our Mom was just serendipity and nothing more besides!

Twenty

My long-standing buddy Vince resides in the UK. From time to time, we exchange correspondence and he keeps me updated and up to speed on what's going on in the old country.

Years ago, Vince and yours truly duetted around youth clubs and 'worse for wear' bars in our home town. Recently, Vince wrote to me saying that ever since Buddy's tragic passing, there were literally dozens of Holly tributes springing up all over the country. He finished by wisecracking: 'there's room for us yet Ricky'!

Back in Ontario, and a departure from the original Holly star-studded line-up; Elroy had incorporated both Lynn and Sherry as my female support vocalists. Our somewhat tardy inception into the schmaltzy music business had somehow grown wings and began to mushroom! What's more, what began as a workaday trio eager to rake in a few spondulicks was, of late, becoming a proficient group; enough to be auditioning for a spot on 'Hamilton's Sunday Party' on channel 11. Not to be left out, local radio was sniffing around too!

Ricky Dale's

Twenty-one

An unconventional feature when the three of us were on stage, is that between numbers the girls would oftentimes josh with the audience. Lynn was particularly top-notch at flawlessly imitating the legendary yodels of the great Hank Williams. Each and every single time, some of their deliberately clumsy skylarking had a tendency to bring the house down. Whilst, on the other hand, Ricky Dale had sort of unwittingly become the 'straight' man, providing the girls with more opportunities to tease and take the mickey out of my so-called coolness. There just couldn't have been a more fun pair to work with – particularly their clever ad-libs I enjoyed.

With regard to 'coolness'; many of Sherry's swanky 'alma mater' acquaintances (many of whom were accustomed to dropping names of chic stores, as easily as Sherry could rattle off obscure singers!) just unreservedly adored her. They often referred to her as being 'cool'. Sherry once told me that she much preferred not to be known as 'cool' – said it was simply a beatnik euphemism with angst!

As time went by, I was kind of relieved that Sherry's current friends and acquaintances were of a generation and social standing, who were completely unaware of Sherry's background. Inasmuch that they were oblivious and ignorant to the fact that Sherry's father killed folks for a living!

However, familiarity with certain ignoramuses caused my Lynn to evaluate her recent showcasing. Apparently, some guy in her class, who had watched her stage act, had become out of line. Inasmuch his annoying habit of leering was making her feel 'denigrated'. She cried inconsolably when telling me; he asked outright to go 'all the way' with her! That same day in the school cafeteria his nose, by chance, collided with my knuckles! The Dean, I hear, wasn't too pleased!

I recall years ago when my Lynn was a little tacker, she was really into her poets and novelists. They became my sister's open space for a fantasy of words. A reserved space behind closed doors where she was safe to conquer things that only exist in the imagination. An exercise of freedom, a defiance against all tyrants, all absurd ideologies and ultimately that of the world with itself

Perhaps in many aspects, Lynn's long-ago muse, could be an idolatry for many of us; particularly as we grow older: Extroversion v introversion?

Ricky Dale's

NOW THAT I AM EIGHTEEN

I've been waiting all this time
Thinking that the world was waiting
Just beyond my world for me.

What did I expect to find?
Something more than what I see
Even if that something is only me!

Twenty-two

Although the popularity of Lynn, Sherry and Ricky as a group of three musicians never lost its strength or momentum – or even tailed-off for an instant, it had become obvious to us that we were progressing in different directions.

Ricky was being primarily sought after for (to a greater extent) corporate engagements. Venues where sublime ballads are the preference and where the singer is principally background. Whereas Lynn and Sherry were extremely versatile as both a main or supporting act, where the audience like to participate at times. Novelty songs such as 'Hot Diggity, Dog Ziggity, Boom"! They go down a treat.

And so, it came to pass and was amicably settled that although we chose to disband, Elroy would still continue to look after both of our interests. Elroy suggested that perhaps from time to time – if the occasion demanded – we could temporarily reform.

For the time being at least, Elroy had secured me a yearly contract as second vocalist at the acclaimed Brant Inn in Burlington, Ontario. Elroy was thoroughly smitten by his part in landing me the contract. Told me that I would no doubt get the opportunity to sing with Lombardo, Kenton and Les Brown orchestras. I had no idea at that time in my career that the aforementioned orchestras were much more than just high falutin' names!

The girls had done well too. Elroy had negotiated a regular spot for them on Steve Allen's TV show. Elroy said that an 'insider' had mentioned that the small NY based Cadence Records was going to be putting out tentative feelers to him, with regard to a recording session with 'his' girls!

Kiss Me Deadly

Dreams can run to reality
And once or twice
Reality works
Though in the end
Reality can dissolve
Completely into dreams.

Ricky Dale's

Twenty-three – Part 1

Everyone has a childhood sweetheart; and she was mine!

I still feel dazed now, when I think of how she looked, standing outside the Brant Inn in the glowing neon. She was an absolutely heavenly human being and of all the stars who came and went during my four years at the Brant, none kindled the love and affection of everyone that she did.

Three months earlier she had arrived by helicopter at Eastwood Park in Hamilton, Ontario, on a promotional tour of the city and now, at the present time, July 4th, 5th and 6th, 1963, she belonged to the Brant and me!

The very first time that I breathed the same air as her was when she wandered leisurely backstage and into my poky changing room. Perhaps she thought it was the John! I'd just finished my early performance and was in the process of putting on a clean shirt at the time. My abashed blushing was stupid, but she just smiled at me and said 'will you sing falling in love again; in a helpless timbre' she added. I had my shirt

Kiss Me Deadly

buttoned up by now and replied 'Mr Anderson (he was the owner of the Brant Inn) won't allow me carte blanche to sing whatever I want to'. She gave me that unique smile of hers and, overacting the part, replied 'I implore you Ricky – it's my most liked song'. In a kind of meticulous manner, she mushed my hair and I guess that was my prompt to sing – and so I did!

It all seemed over and done so quickly and as she turned to go; she asked me 'why do you work in a place like this Ricky?' I didn't really grasp an answer, so I simply replied 'I enjoy the articulation' … 'me too' she replied; and left. Just before my 'solo', she had taken a book from her gemstone clutch bag and offered it to me 'I'd like you to have it' she said seriously.

Sitting bolt upright on the threadbare old Chesterfield and holding the gift she had presented me with earlier, I purposely flicked swiftly through the pages until I found the exact verse I was looking for: 'In the people whom we love, there is, imminent a certain dream which we cannot always clearly define.'[4]

---

[4] Jayne Mansfield was an incomparable lady who if she so wished could either ruin a person's entire perception of life or, alternatively, make a person so ecstatically happy. And she chose to alight upon me! But how on earth could she have been aware that long ago Bunin's poetry had seeped into my being and that I adored her to distraction because of it?

Ricky Dale's

I was born when she arrived
I died when she departed.
I lived for three short days
While I loved her.

Twenty-three – Part 2

I guess that this 'Part 2' is my forlorn epitaph to a greatly revered lady!

I would dearly love to recount to my valued reader of how one evening I had inundated Jayne with red roses and, in addition, we had a candlelit supper. However, sad to say it didn't happen! Nonetheless there was no question that we at the Brant would not be the zenith of her tour.

After she left Hamilton for Burlington, the Hamilton Spectator's headline read as follows:

'Today she's gone leaving a 41-18-35½ inch gap on the Hamilton skyline'.

Although it served as a great publicity headline for Jayne's Brant Inn engagement, I truly hated all of the yatter, yatter regarding her 'body'. I felt that there was a certain sadness about it – like it had a tendency to make her sound sinful!

Folks who grew up in the roaring 1920s, like Zelda

and Scott Fitzgerald, they all had held unrestrained pleasure-bent lives. This would eventually mould the shape and lives of a new generation. It was into this generation that Vera Jane Palmer was born on April 19th 1933.

John Dillinger was still making headlines and Darryl Zanuck, who would one day make Jayne a star, had just become production chief of Warner Brothers.

Gangster films were the vogue; Marlene Dietrich began wearing trousers and film idols were, among others, Mae West, Jean Harlow, Clark Gable, Katherine Hepburn and Spencer Tracy.

Jayne grew up fascinated by movies; she told me that she had seen her very first motion picture when she was just six years of age:

'I came home from school and used to imitate the stars in some of their scenes, acting them out in front of a large mirror in my momma's bedroom. I knew I was going to be a movie star someday. Momma would laugh when I told her that I was "going to be famous for both of us".'

And, in due course, she was!

Kiss Me Deadly

Twenty-four

It was just before Christmas 1964; just several days after Martin Luther King Jr accepted the Nobel Peace Prize and restated his belief that non-violent methods could create a world in which 'none shall be afraid'.

On the nights that Sherry wasn't in bed before I got home late, she would sprint through our apartment just as soon as she heard the car in the driveway. I know this to be so because one night, in her excitable fluster, she bashed her pinkie toe on the fire grate surround. She'd wrap her arms around my neck and her legs around my waist and snog my stubbled fizzog to bits, squawking 'Ricky, Ricky'. I'd hold her tight for several eternities; never, ever tiring of it.

Dear reader: Yes indeed, Sherry and yours truly did ultimately get hitched when she turned eighteen in July 1964, and I am so much better for it!

Despite being edged onto the 'Hot 100' list and being offered a lucrative contract on the college concert circuit, the public's appetite for more of them had an unsettling effect on both Lynn and Sherry, more than you could imagine.

All they hankered for was just an iota of normalcy in their manic lives. And so, approximately 10 months later, they began to satisfy any of their contractual obligations and in doing so cocked a snook at the demanding music scene; for the ultimate betterment of themselves!

With regard to Sherry – me and her were hankering for a baby and were going for it lickety-split. And, as luck would have it, it seemed that God's grace had shined upon us!

My dear 'doppelganger' Lynn had never been a person who was dissatisfied with the cards she had been dealt. On the contrary, and similar in nature as myself, she was a very positive thinking person. She did, however, have two vulnerabilities; first, she insisted on wearing clothes with a plunging neckline! Second, her absence from the old country was getting the better of her – indeed she wanted to go 'home'. I'd seen her trying to keep a brave face and pine away at the same time!

Lynn's send-off was a tearful occasion at The Winter Creek Inn. Family, of course, but not only family – customers too, were all cut from the same cloth. Inasmuch that nobody had a hankering to lose dear Lynn to the old country – we all felt that she had paid her incomer dues and, as such, she now belonged here with us!

Having said that, I absolutely would swear on oath that there was at least one occasion, that emotional evening when I thought my Lynn might rescind her decision – have a change of heart – so to speak. Be that as it may, within 24 hours she had left Manhattan docks and was on the high seas back to Blighty!

Despite all of that, one thing was for certain. Lynn was going to fall short of toasting our mom's 'maple syrup pie' for some time. It seems to me that half the pleasure of settling into a new country is the tasting of unusual food, or eating dishes that you might already know, but they are cooked in a somewhat different fashion. For sure, eating and watching your waist line, do not necessarily go hand in hand in North America. A continent far removed from the British Isles – a continent that has more than its fair share of delicious victuals on offer, especially desserts and cakes! So, for those of you who lack the willpower to refuse; try out the aforementioned **Mom's Maple Syrup Pie!**

1 cup maple syrup
⅓ cup water
3 tbsp corn starch
2 tbsp butter
⅓ cup nuts (Grenoble or pecan)
Your favourite pie crust

Ricky Dale's

Bring to boil maple syrup and water. Mix corn starch with a little water, pour into boiling syrup, stir well until mixture is nice and smooth. Add butter and nuts according to taste. Pour into 9-inch pie dish, cover with some pie crust. Make small cuts on top. Bake at 190°C (375°F), gas mark 5, for 20 to 30 minutes. Serves 4 – Enjoy!

Kiss Me Deadly

Twenty-five

And what of my Sherry and me?
Sherry's father wasn't accustomed to explaining the whys and wherefores of a situation, or accountable for his actions and expected to explain them too. And, therefore, when Sherry handed me a set of keys for a two-bedroom apartment, I didn't wince at all about it. Sherry said that, in response to our just gone nuptials, he'd decided he didn't want us living at The Winter Creek Inn any longer. It was a nice, spacious apartment and even included a crib room for the newborn.

The organisation owned and ran a succession of laundromats along the lake shore from Toronto though Hamilton. Each had its own self-contained living accommodation. Ours was situated in Burlington and extremely convenient to my work at the Brant Inn. The only drawback was that, in order to enter the apartment, access was through the laundromat.

You may recall 'Mr Stoneface', the Edward G.

Ricky Dale's

Robinson guy who chauffeured my Sherry to and from her work at The Winter Creek Inn. In actual fact he was quite an affable fellow and even arranged for some goons to assist with the furniture removals to our new location. I expect you guessed that chauffeuring wasn't entirely his line of work. He was Sherry's Pop's bodyguard and soldier – exclusively!

We settled into our new home like a dream – it was hard to comprehend that in just 12 weeks we would become three! Initially Sherry and I were more than pleased to live at Winter Creek. Elroy had even refurbished a small cabin for us (used by summer vacation folk).

Elroy was knowledgeable regarding Sherry's family and recommended we should not bitch about her father's 'offer' as such. Elroy hinted that the family were known to become incredibly 'edgy' when events didn't go as planned! I'm relieved that Elroy is majorly versed in these matters of Cosa Nostra and such. It seems to me that we Devon dumplings are only endowed with a certain naivety. Nightmarish going-on are not our strong point at all.

There is much moaning and groaning and jabbering among law enforcement officers regarding as to whether the so-called Mafia or Cosa Nostra is, as such, non-existent; because that's the way it has been described for many decades. For example, the roots of the trade in heroin and cocaine, in which many western countries are now enmeshed. Remain buried, out of sight – no more than a mirage of yesteryear. The general view today that it was Lansky and Luciano that set the Mafia down the road in an organised way, now seems to be boringly 'old hat'.

One of the problems with suggesting that Montreal is the Mafia capital of Canada, is finding out beforehand. For example, you must know whether you are dealing with a potential heavy-weight contender, or perhaps just a heavy-weight! It seems to me that is precisely what law enforcement has failed to do. Speculation that Cosa Nostra, as such, is merely a tool of a shadowy figure, the guiding hand of a mysterious puppet-master, is certainly fanciful at best!

Ricky Dale's

Twenty-six

Hamilton got hammered on Sunday by a savage lake-effect snowstorm that dumped 37 inches in 6 hours, one of the heaviest snowfalls the city has ever seen in one day. The second largest storm in the city's history moved in at around 4pm and dropped more than 3 feet of new snow on top of the record totals already on the ground, shutting down streets, offices and the airport. Densely, laborious heaven-sent snow all over the map. Looked to me as though every man jack and his brood would be out tobogganing up till late as midnight!

However, it meant not one iota to my bewitching spouse, who had an overwhelming ambition to go out cruising in our newly acquired 1959 Ford Thunderbird convertible. Which on good authenticity, we had been told that the admired Frankie Avalon had been the previous owner!

My Sherry: 100% love and pure photogenic magic. Waist length jet black hair and, even at 18 going on 19, zilch baby fat. How could this poor captive refuse her invitation?!

It was all-important for her to show off our 'famous' and newly acquired vehicle to Dad Zito at the Golden Gloves – so that's where we were heading right now! Dad Zito wasn't even halfway pleased to see us, 'especially in these appalling conditions' he irritatingly reminded us. Without changing the vitriolic expression on his face, he chided us to return to Burlington forthwith; garage the vehicle and hire a cab for work that evening. Hindsight is a luxury for some, for others it can be a life changer. Be that as it may, Dad Zito was all there with his advice, that horrid day!

Ricky Dale's

I dream of the falling, falling snow,
A candle flame,
Shadows on the wall,
The chill of your lips,
Wet hair and cold toes,
And the warmest embrace.

Kiss Me Deadly

Twenty-seven

Although Mr Lombardo was somewhat mean to me, credit where credit is due. Inasmuch that New Year's Eve simply wasn't New Year's Eve until you've heard the Guy Lombardo Band playing Auld Lang Syne! Old acquaintances were rarely forgotten whenever Guy Lombardo and his Royal Canadians played the Brant Inn. Quite simply, the Lombardo Orchestra was the Brant Inn's most popular attraction; appearing nine times between 1952 and 1962. Usually for four evenings on each visit.

I was an absolutely wet behind the ears kid when I was first invited to sing with Mr Lombardo's prestigious band. He was from the old school of meticulous maestros – he was so precise and accurate about even minor details. Oftentimes when, frustratingly, I didn't come up to par, he would bawl at me. It's true that at the time I did indescribably loath the man. However, upon reflection he absolutely taught Ricky Dale the trade – and pretty much everything I know am likely to know – in this life!

Ricky Dale's

Unquestionably it was twofold frustrating for Mr Lombardo to have to tolerate 'Ricky Dale'. Inasmuch that he was obliged to be hamstrung with me on account of Dad Zito calling the shots at the Brant Inn. There are most probably many retirees today that do not have a notion that the beloved Brant Inn was indeed under Mafia control.

What bugged me most of all was the schmaltzy songs that he insisted I sing. Not even to mention the way in which he would demandingly point and wave his baton at me: for my benefit only!

Years later my criticism seems somewhat putrid. In all honesty and, put in the simplest terms, Guy Lombardo and Ricky Dale made the best possible sense of the situation as it was, we acknowledged the status quo, and just got on with our work ... eventually!

The understanding between teacher and pupil goes beyond just drawing the butterfly out of its chrysalis at times!

Kiss Me Deadly

Twenty-eight

Getting myself all clobbered-up and looking as chic and dapper as a new age James Dean was one of my overriding principles. My self-assurance to professionally perform was very dependent upon it. The process wouldn't be quick; however, this evening I'd already decided to wear my most snappy suit, and Sherry had agreed too. A couple of months ago she'd taken one of my regular suits in hand and sewed mother-of-pearl gemstones on the lapels and the trousers too. She'd been trimming my hair for the past several months and insisted that she wanted me to sport a (beastly!) Beatle cut.

I'd done the New Year's Eve bash for the first-time last year; however, Mr Lombardo wanted us all to arrive a shade early in order to quickly run through the schedule and such. I wanted to have a beer with my new buddy Chico Fernandez too. Chico was an exceptionally easy-going guy. He was kind of hooked on British bands. However, this evening he'd be drumming up a storm with the Royal Canadians

– the whole caboodle of them!

It was more than likely to be past 2am before we'd finished 'Happy New Year' and kissing everyone. With that in mind my Sherry had decided to invite her old school pal Frances to come around to our apartment for supper and stay over too. Frances had recently become estranged from husband Joe – it was a really short-lived marriage.

Drifting back to my mention of the Royal Canadians in Lombardo's band. They honestly reminded me more of bank managers than musicians. Chico and I were really the babes of the outfit in comparison with the others – who were middle-aged men! And drifting back again to the subject of babes. The new tradition of late was the midnight arrival of a diapered toddler bursting through the paper face of a large clock on the upper bandstand – that was really imaginative!

Kiss Me Deadly

Was your day filled with wanting or the needle point of knowing I waited
          For you?

          I did.
          I do.

Ricky Dale's

Twenty-nine

After all of the ballyhoo leading toward New Year's Eve, the final arrangements allowed for me to sing just three songs all evening! Nonetheless though, whilst I was waiting for my signal in the wings, a commissary advised me of a telephone call from Stan Kenton (Kenton Orchestra). I was able to immediately return the call and was overjoyed to learn that they wanted me to audition for them early in the new year. Apparently, they require a vocalist for seven or eight tracks on a forthcoming long-playing album being produced!

The evening at the Brant did go swimmingly well though. And astonishingly I was authorised to sing the whole evening out with my own rendition of Auld Lang Syne. Not one of Mr Lombardo's insensitive criticisms after the event either!

By the time the Brant had said 'goodnight' to its patrons and opened its main doors – to let the cold in – folks were already lined up the stairs and beyond. As they spilled out into the bitter night, Chico and I made a wise decision to sit the rush out in the Sky Club lounge. News was filtering in that dozens of the New Year's Eve revellers had become stranded in their automobiles and had to wait patiently for emergency vehicles and road crews with snowploughs to rescue them.

Ed Krekowski, Owner of Ed's Garage on Chippewa Street, had just popped into the Brant for a quick snorter before he began his towing 'obligations': 'One wrong move on these streets and you're stuck for good – it's a Godless labyrinth out there' he said very knowledgeably.

A posse of Ontario Provincial Police joined us in the lounge. They had obviously just been involved in some sort of catastrophe. All of them were absolutely flecked by the fast-falling snow – even in the heat of the lounge it was not melting immediately on their wet clothes. The sergeant-at-arms blurted out: 'Person killed outright on Queen Elizabeth Way'. 'Whiteout' I enquired. 'Drink driver responsible' he replied unsmiling. 'Vehicle was broadsided by a paralytic driver in a pickup truck – just at the top of Maple and First. I could throttle the SOB, I really could' said the other provincial cop disparagingly.

Hot coffee and donuts had now become the order of the day. The sergeant-at-arms had begun to unravel for us exactly what had occurred that evening: 'The tragedy came about 1am. The DD jumped the red

Ricky Dale's

light and careered at speed into the nearside of an old '59 Thunderbird. Two young women in the 'bird'. One is DOA, the other, our only witness, is mainly shaken-up'. Chico was more honed than me – he was sharp, I heard him breath faintly ''59 Thunderbird'.

Kiss Me Deadly

Thirty

A state of deep and quiet calm transfixed the intensity of my smashed reasoning and strength of feeling and response.

Even to this day, I cannot recollect how I managed to manoeuvre myself out of the Brant. I do recall a lot of people fussing and Chico trying to persuade me to come home with him. But that's about all I recall. I didn't even seem to struggle in walking the four long blocks home to our apartment. It was as though as long as I kept walking, nothing would attempt to be real! I could still unmistakenly overhear Sherry's passive voice on our telephone, imploring Frances to 'come on over, The Beverley Hillbillies Christmas Special is on, and Ricky's bought us a new colour TV!'

Rounding the corner to our laundromat apartment, some folks, I strangely recollect, were actually doing a wash load! Whilst outside happy groups of party-goers were profusely singing their hearts out. Neighbourhood dogs joining in with a hodgepodge of incomprehensible hubbub! Me too, I wanted to add to the disarray by shamefacedly making a long, loud piercing scream until my lungs were in a state of collapse. But who would want to hear – and what good would it do anyway?

Dementedly on my hands and knees, moving slowly forward up the concrete staircase to our would-be refuge. 30° below on the streets and I'm breaking out in sweats of anxiety and distress – body blenching inconsolably. It was as though my new half-witted self had taken over – that I'd gone soft in the head; because unintelligently when I arrived at the top of the stairs, I began listening for her voice at the closed front door! Perhaps she is deathless, immortal – would she recognise me, would she know me of old?

The large wooden front door opens by the immutable constant that only doors themselves know! Across our passageway, in the motionless mirror, I can't help briefly glimpse the outline of my pitiful wretched face – a mask of despondence; half hiding, half revealing. I hear Sherry's clear falsetto tone, asking me, begging me over and over to tell her who we have become! Her voice becomes louder; she is shouting at me now; telling me straight and unrelentingly, not to ever allow her to go again, not unless I intend to go too!

Kiss Me Deadly

The memory of a love long ago is like the old grey sweater with holes that I keep telling myself I'll throw away
Someday,
Not today though
I still need it
And tomorrow too!

Ricky Dale's

Thirty-one

I've heard folks comment that immediately a person leaves this world there is oftentimes a kind of malignancy that permeates their abode. Not so! My Sherry always had an odourless scent about her. Perhaps best described as a squeaky-clean smell tinged with clementines. I guess that's the reason why I never want to leave this apartment again; I can smell her here; right now; an inviting 'ultraviolet magnetism' of sorts unleashed and smothering me to bits!

I returned to the real world really quick, when I became extremely conscious of size 12 snow-boots clumping up the laundromat stairs toward our apartment. Sounded as though the devil incarnate was looking for lost souls and was about to express his surprise and annoyance at yours truly remaining cognisant and continuing to exist! Possibly an accurate assumption, inasmuch that the rowdy visitor was the big fella, was the person who Sherry and me had christened Edward G!

'Edward G' had been associated with high-ranking mafioso and their lieutenants for longer than most folks remember. After a brief apprenticeship smuggling moonshine liquor from Kentucky, he went on to act as arbitrator in many of the Mafia wars. After serving time for income tax evasion, the Zito family snapped him up as their 'inquisitor chief'. An extremely lucrative and flexible title!

When he spoke, you paid attention. When he said 'sit down kid', I pricked up my ears and did just that! It was an order, and I listened to his every word: 'It is a sorrowful tragedy what happened to Candelaria. I'd known her since she was a baby and she matured into a beautiful woman. The Zito family are overwhelmed with grief'. He had a slow way of looking at folk through his thick black eyebrows that, to be candid, gave me the heebie-jeebies! He continued: 'It seems to me that you ought to know that the miscreant, who was responsible, has already gone to meet his maker'. He followed the last sentence by conveying something in Italian. Whatever he had said, the grimace on his face implied something of a very unpleasant nature! He added: 'Fortunately the OPPs had allowed him bail, which the Zito family paid, and notified me'. 'What of Frances – the passenger' I enquired. 'She is little Miss Fortunate' he replied, and proceeded to give me the important facts: 'The pick-up truck jumped a red light and slammed into the driver's side door. The passenger side of the vehicle where little Miss Fortunate was sat, didn't take a knock. Apparently, your wife was wanting to secretly take you by surprise whilst Auld Lang Syne was being romped around with. Some surprise, eh?!'

> Heavy-headed, staring down avoiding
> Yuletide smiles and New Year promise, I stay
> as calm as crystal, but I am still afraid of
> looking up.

Kiss Me Deadly

Thirty-two

I knew this steely-eyed old pro was noticeably trying to find the up-and-go enthusiasm to alert me to something life-changing. His face and mannerism were not unlike when our Mom told us kids that our Dad wouldn't be coming home again! Although the way in which he finally uncorked the announcement still left me in disbelief and somewhat flummoxed by the outcome. Pretty much, this is how he told it to me: 'When this head-to-head is finished, you are going to catch your breath and catch the next available Amtrak to NY, ok?!' At this very instant your Achilles heel is the Zito family who, although I haven't been given the go-ahead yet, are going to want you eliminated soon. The way in which Rocco justifies your demise, is being 100% certain that you, Ricky Dale, are solely accountable for his daughter's death. He claims that "you", my friend, had asked his Cadelaria to fetch "you" from the Brant Inn just after midnight. The stumbling block for "you" Ricky, is that Rocco's word is final!'

He seemed to punctuate his sentences a lot by using the expression 'my friend'. I was positive that the reference wasn't a literal one, however, it helped to assure me that perhaps he was on my side – at least I wasn't going to be murkily murdered in the short term at least! He finished by adding: 'It's only a matter of perhaps several hours before arrangements are forthcoming for your disposal. This is an improper advance tip-off that damn quick you need to pack your valise and skedaddle, preferably back to the UK my friend! Your wife would understand my friend – so do it for her. You need to go now or otherwise you will be gone! I'll convey you to Union Railway Station straight away!'

Strange the things that enter a person's mind when their life is on the line. What kept going through my head was how I'd never had a butchers at our extremely overpriced colour TV set – for that matter, neither had my cherished Sherry!

Thirty-three

Edward G and yours truly, parted company without even a handshake or a 'bon voyage'. Inasmuch that he'd given me my life, the 'cheerio' niceties were of no great importance.

I was fortunate enough not to have a long wait before Amtrak came swiftly to my rescue. Super quick I arrived at Penn Station in Manhattan. Everything seemed so erratic and surreal – images mixed together that were complicated and difficult to fathom out. I am ever so madly and passionately in love with a girl called Sherry – indeed she is my wife. Then justify for me, what am I doing here in Manhattan without her here beside me?

My whole nightmare would have been somewhat less fraught and traumatically draining had I been in a position to tell Mom and Elroy what had taken place and my reason for a hurried exit. It will be a hellish shout when the truth of Rocco's revenge is revealed, I guess they will hear all about the chain of events in due course. It was a big weight off though when I realised we'd crossed over Rainbow Bridge into the United States. Although a false security inasmuch a bullet is directional and tends to ignore borders!

I headed for the Taft Hotel[5] in the midtown Manhattan neighbourhood. Sherry and I used to enjoy staying there whenever either of us had an overnight gig in the city. I can confess though that, on this occasion, I was so relieved to have gotten out of that NY taxi cab. I adore those yatter, yatter cabbies usually, however this guy was so in awe of those blasted Beatles. It's 'thorny' being English at times!

2,250 rooms at the Taft Hotel. RD felt a sense of security being finally tucked away in one of them. I put the light out, climbed into the super king size bed, pulled the bedclothes firmly around me, and crashed out into a world of Sherry and Ricky!

---

5   The Taft became The Michelangelo in recent years.

Kiss Me Deadly

Thirty-four

Remembering Sherry the Sinatra way.

It was winter in Manhattan.
Falling snowflakes filled the air.
The streets were covered with a film of ice.
But a little simple magic
That I'd heard about somewhere
Changed the weather all around us.

The day that I bought her violets for her fur.
And it was spring for a while remember?
I bought her violets for her fur
And there was April in that December.

The snow drifted down on the flowers
And that's where it lay.
The snow looked like dew on the blossom
As on a summer day.

The day that I bought her violets for her fur
There was blue in the winter sky
Then she pinned my violets to her fur
And gave a lift to the crowds passing by.

Ricky Dale's

You smiled at me so sweetly
Since then, one thought occurs
That we fell in love completely
The day that I bought her violets for her fur.

Thirty-five

I sat around the hotel lounge most of the next day, just trying to factorise my life. Smoking 'Luckys' and drinking coffee was all I had the strength and energy to fit my needs. I guess it served a purpose because the next day (the morning of January 3rd) I was up with the lark, showered and making my way down to the wharf diner. I had heard said that the SS America on pier 11 was going to be taking on passengers today. She had been laid up since September due to a union issue but was now getting ready to set sail again.

Customarily there's a strike every now and then. The good news was that the shipping line had been obliged to take on a crew of foreign workers; brought in by the union – none of whom would be clued-up on sagas such as mine!

If you are willing to take what's available, it's never problematic finding a passage on a UK bound liner. I was able to share quite a spacious cabin with three other guys – German, French and Spanish – all of whom could only speak pigeon English Fortunately no person of Italian descent though! One of the guys quipped, in his broken English, that we all were equivalent to the League of Nations.[6]

Two full days at sea and, late one evening, I was handed a printed 'shore to ship' telegraph message by our attendant/steward. Its drift was crystal clear and read as follows: 'You have disappointed me!' It was signed *Rocco Zito*.

> A thousand doors have closed. Behind them an iron silence has fallen. A thousand lights have switched off. In their empty sockets a heavy silence has opened its eyes, and looked deeply into mine!

---

6   Superseded by the United Nations.

Thirty-six

They grow old and people grow tired: they forget. Rocco forgot the rights and wrongs of the sorrowful tragedy of his daughter Candelaria losing her life. As far as he was concerned someone needed to be answerable. He was from a very old school, and he quite clearly believed that what he intended to do to me was not only for the loss of his daughter, but also for the compromised honour of the old days and ways, the old Cosa Nostra.

On the basis of that I needed to keep a very low profile and not attract any attention, even though I would soon be back in the UK.

Whilst onboard ship my intuitive sense of false of security was telling me that I was fundamentally out of harm's way. Withall in the event that my execution was such a priority, why forward a shore to ship telegram message – isn't that, in fact, showing your hand? That said as well; it seems to me an extremely more fitting place to dispose of my body, would be odds-on, by tossing it overboard in the mid-Atlantic!

Ricky Dale's

What really gnawed at me the most was whether or not they intended to hand out my just desserts at the Southampton dockside after I had disembarked. My awful sneaking suspicion is that was what they have in mind!

Ode to Candelaria

I'm afraid it will be hard to recognise you
when I die.
Shouldn't be too difficult though;
Only you have the habit of hiding and
talking to me behind silly words about
things I never wanted to learn about.
For instance: planting a walnut tree in grass
and watering it,
With rain from your hair!

Ricky Dale's

Thirty-seven

The SS America completed its 7-day Atlantic crossing and came into port at Southampton around 7pm. Apparently it had been used as a troop ship during WW2. Passenger initials and such had been whittled into many of the handrails. In view of the fact that none of my family know of my whereabouts, perhaps I should have left my own moniker too – 'Ricky' instead of 'Kilroy', eh?!

The British contingent was able to whiz through customs double quick (dual nationality has its benefits!) and all the glories of a wet Southampton street in January were mine! I was watching and assuming the worst. However, tail between my legs, I lived to fight another day – 'not tonight Josephine' sprung to mind!

My taxicab driver suggested the Polygon Hotel as a nice central location and that, indeed, was to become my home for the foreseeable future. I booked in under the handle of 'Lucas Doolin'. He had been a character played by the superb Robert Mitchum in the movie 'Thunder Road'. Sounded like a cool and impregnable title to me.

Thirty-eight

I could never have imagined a situation so utterly bizarre as hiding out in one's own country. Not only but also fearing that a nondescript gunsel has me on his 'to do' list.

More or less a fortnight has passed since my beloved Sherry was killed and the hurt is still very much a part of every hour of my life. I cannot get any respite whilst the Zito family refuse to acknowledge my explanation of blamelessness. It seems to me that I am as fuddled and stunned as I am ever likely to be so, with that in mind, perhaps I should be more favourable to the way things stand!

It was in my long association with my Sherry's family, that I became totally aware of what Rocco was capable of. The overall power in making antagonists disappear was his forte and Edward G was his proficiency in the accomplishment of such tasks. I've been aware of stuff going on but it was none of my business. I was Sherry's husband; period!

When I was onboard ship, I had little to do, and spent a lot of my time looking out to sea and truly challenging me, myself to figure out what exactly is happening here – is there some ulterior underlying reason? It crossed my mind several times that perhaps conceivably the Zito heads are running somewhat scared; inasmuch that since Candelaria is no longer Ricky Dale's attachment to the 'family', the speculation is that he could become a loose cannon; and as such he has the feasible intent to cause harm to the family!

Perhaps it's not a question of me being responsible for the death of Candelaria but, moreover, it's a question of me not having a strong alliance with the family since her death. In other words, me being alive tends to make them the vulnerable party!

A Sketch Of My Great Utopia

Whilst
The barrel of a gun
Chillingly licks
My neck
And hisses in my ear
The command is
To be happy

Ricky Dale's

Thirty-nine

RD decided that the best strategy available, under the circumstances, was indubitably for him to 'play dead'. For the undesirable future RD was going to become 'Lucas Doolin' until further notice. I have found that oftentimes life has its small salvations. In this instance it took a Southampton attorney only 45 minutes to formalise a change of name document/certificate and Lucas Doolin was born. A very stress-free birth too!

Puts me in mind of the two main characters on TV's The Patty Duke Show. They are identical cousins, both, of course, played by Patty. Special effect being relatively primitive in the era in question, meant that each time zany, all American, forever in a fix, but good-hearted Patty Lane faced the camera to talk to her prim Scottish-born cousin Cathy, someone had to stand with her back to the camera and pretend to be Cathy, and when it was Cathy's turn to show her face, someone had to play Patty!

I trust that it won't be as complicated as that for Lucas Doolin and Ricky Dale, eh?!

Forty

I had a notion to quit Southampton and relocate to my old home town in Devon. I wasn't sure whether or not this was a sensible thing to do, inasmuch that here in the city it's easy for a person to remain anonymous, whereas in the countryside everybody knows who you are. The other complication being that the law of averages would assume that Sherry had mentioned our Devonshire roots to Pop Zito and, therefore, a move to Devon would give him a head start! I missed not having an audience too. However, even if I limited myself to just small gigs, it could get me killed really quick!

The following years seemed to fly by, and memories of being a youngster in my own home town were always very wistfully present. I didn't want those nostalgic thoughts to be a literal cause of my death but, on the other hand, I'd tired of being a pussycat and I was going home. I could hear my Sherry commending me: 'Be released my Ricky, go home!'

The precious part of my own personal world,

the log-awaited move was over. Although upon reflection, the actuality of what was taking place differed somewhat from the dream-filled concept that I'd held in my head for years. War baby versus Generation X. Who knows, eh?!

My Lynn had been at my side non-stop whilst I was 'exiled' in Southampton. With regard to covering our tracks, her inventiveness was way ahead of mine and it would truly warrant another book to put into words what she has accomplished! We both are of the opinion that the interim period has been long enough to give us an element of protection; we hope, we hope!

Kiss Me Deadly

Then it was time,
Time to arrive
A few years late,
And time to begin
Perhaps where we left off
So many years ago
In a different place.

And you know it's
Never too late
To begin again, because
The thrill of being home
Gripped me almost like pain.

Ricky Dale's

Forty-one

Lynn and I were overjoyed that we'd finally made a firm resolution to relocate to Devon, and straight away too! We maintained that our Mom was a perfect example of how to be successful as a restauranteur; particularly taking on a rundown, neglected business too.

In any event running a restaurant and entertaining had, for the most part, been the predominant pursuit of our adult lives. In an attempt to avoid Zito's wrath, attention seeking pursuits such as entertaining were out!

Sufficient to add that if our Mom can make it in Canada, we ought to be able to make a go right here in the UK. With that in mind, we foraged around Devon for some such rough diamond of a catering business, that had potential, if turned upside down and inside out, to become a seriously flourishing business.

It was sooner, rather than later, that we were fated to stumble upon the very same lame duck we'd been searching for. A tired and sick eating establishment in a cute Devon shopping locality – just calling out to us! We bid for it and we bought it. It was perfect for us and we just snapped it up!

With regard to the troublesome Rocco Zito; he and his henchmen seemed a lifetime away. En route to our heaven in Devon, we'd managed to shut those murderous punks right out of our consciousness; at least, seemingly so!

Lynn and I oftentimes would speak in a joking way about our close connection with the Zitos. We'd laugh and refer to them as 'The Pizza Connection!'[7]

---

[7] The Pizza Connection, as far as American law enforcement was concerned, began when 82 kilos of heroin was discovered on New York's docks. Customs agents arrested a man who turned out to run a pizza joint. In fact, all the evidence in the case seemed to have some connection with pizzas and pizzeria operators!

Ricky Dale's

Forty-two

Do you sometimes identify a specific period or day in your own life, by bringing it into line with that of a specific moment in world events? For example: Gerald Ford declared that he would no longer preside over the 'decline and fall of the United States'. The new president, southerner Jimmy Carter, pre-empted by saying America was 'sick at heart and needed faith'. And by that same token, in the bleak fall of 1976, it was coming up to our fifth anniversary of the opening of Lynn and Ricky's restaurant! Lynn and talked about the 'happening' for many years and really wanted us to have a big bash – 'almost as if it was a movie premiere first night or such', she oftentimes said knowingly optimistically.

There was little doubt in either of our minds that we desired the occasion to be something of a unique phenomenon – especially for all of the special friends we had made down here in these South Devon 'boonies'. Lynn had also taken on additional staff and made arrangements for a DJ from the city of

Plymouth, to take over and host the big event. Not only but also, Westward Television Group were sending along one of their anchor persons and presenter too. It was all good and we had earned it!

Tickets were available to those folk not invited with the takings being donated to a good cause. Complementary victuals and drinks were being made available to all well-wishers too!

Ricky Dale's

Twins In A Twinkling
(to my sister Lynn)

I can't normally remember anniversaries,
However, today is our anniversary,
Sorry that I arrived so late, in fear
And made you wonder
If I'd arrive at all!
I did,
A few minutes hence =
And we started
The rest of our lives,
Without a Zito in sight!

Forty-three

Personally, I've never seen stranger-looking folk than those I've seen in Chelsea today. I wish to say that I've seen some very strange folk on Broadway in my day but not at all like those in Chelsea. However, it doesn't stop there, because the dogs are even stranger-looking; big heads and wrinkled faces and big, round eyes that seem so sad I half expected to see them bust out crying!

Long before our celebrations are due to get underway at the end of the week and, with all the extra staff to cope, Lynn and I were determined to treat ourselves, and we booked an overnight excursion, by train to London. In particular, this journey was for the purpose of getting fitted-out with some devilishly chic duds! I bought a nicely tailored black three-piece suit, together with a fedora – its brim cocked down toward one eye. Lynn, on the other hand, chose a really swinging London outfit – I'll illustrate it carefully for you: A white mini which was kind of crosshatched by a barely discernible geometric

Ricky Dale's

print. All finished off by glimmering stockings. Lynn also treated herself to some Mary Quant Chelsea-girl makeup, a simple haircut and oval glasses – she unquestionably looks the cat's pyjamas!

Mini-skirts and pop-art ties are more than modern man can bear. The next thing that Harrods will sell is silver-coated underwear or maybe edible cotton-candy wigs for those who like tattoos on their flabby pecks and foxtails on their motorbikes.

Kiss Me Deadly

Forty-four

Let's talk about makeup. Let's talk about two hours in the makeup chair before each gig. Nine out of ten disc jockeys just wouldn't take the trouble with all that sort of preparation but 'Dave the Dude was the difference between the wheat and the chaff! Dave told me that not only did the making-up and dressing-up make him confident to play the part, but also his audience perception of him as an artist changed too. We'd heard via the grapevine that our Plymouth city disc jockey was somewhat outlandish and wacky. However, we didn't ever want one of those run of the mill moronic characters whose only articulation was putting records on a turntable! I grew to appreciate Dave the Dude as the evening progressed – he told jokes that I hadn't heard before too!

Of course, it wasn't necessary for us to spill the beans to Dave over the change of name thing, and so he innocently recognised me, pretty much straight away, as Ricky Dale. Certainly not as Lucas Doolin, like the rest of our guests! And, of course, nobody knew that a misguided psychotic was contracted to kill Ricky Dale.

Before Dave the Dude had begun his act proper, I decided to take advantage of the jolly antiquated Joanna, stood in the corner of the room, by banging out some of the show tunes Mom had taught me. Folks began singing along and even Westward Television began filming. And dear Dave, getting into the swing of the party and suddenly recalling who I really was, yelled: 'That's Ricky Dale; now sing us one of your old numbers!'

Dave had so unintentionally let the cat out of the bag. It's bizarre how a name from the past can attract people's attention so quickly, especially when the person concerned has been incognito for a decade or so.

Not wishing to be a party-pooper, I gave in to the 'majority' and even agreed to do the celeb autograph thing as well. I must admit that, in many respects, 'coming clean' was a really huge weight off at last!

Forty-five

Lynn and I had planned for this shindig for six glorious weeks, making certain that nothing would be left to chance. We'd even had new carpet put down in the lounge bar. There is nothing like deep pile Wilton underfoot to fill a room with a wonderful feeling of excitement and unreality! Actually, it all went much better than we thought it would – except we weren't likely to be able to escape the clutches of the media. After we'd well and truly paid the piper and, after which, all of the eating, dancing and jollifications had yelled a final whoopee, my dear sister placed her caring arm around my aching shoulders and half-heartedly remarked 'add spunky to our resumé!' She was totally hip, my sister!

I cuddled Lynn close to me, I think we were both on the verge of tears, most probably neck and neck! This time I seemed to do the speaking: 'we've got ourselves a progressive and joyful communal set-up here in the sticks and I don't want us to lose it

– however, it seems to me that we are awfully close to it!'

'The mess and the possible damage that even unpretentious gossip is likely to bring about, doesn't fill me with confidence Lynn. When all at once the 'Ricky Dale' thingummy starts to gain some momentum, both our lives could be at risk! Like a candy bar in the hands of children, the news won't linger on any one pair of lips before it's passed on quickly to another. How long do you think it will be before the Toronto media have it in their group?'

I was really in 'overdrive' now! 'I'm so disgusted with myself for having put you through this tension and emotional manoeuvres, my little sister. I'm whacked out too, with the uncertainty of running from pillar to post. And I'm bored with the title of Lucas Doolin – it's not me, I'm not a Lucas Doolin! Forgive me Lynn but, with all that in mind, I'm heading back to Toronto – in the event that Rocco wants his pound of flesh, then better sooner than later when I'm not expecting it!'

Forty-six

After all that I sounded off about last night, I woke this morning and the only new resolution that crossed my mind was that I'm between a rock and a hard place! I guess, with that in mind, I'm going to drink some coffee and cross the Atlantic before I change my mind again. It was a glorious summer morning. God had made it a technical necessity that it should be so, in case rain stopped play! Ricky made a large pot of coffee and the two of them sat sad and hushed at the pine kitchen table. Lynn stood up, walked around the table to where Ricky was sat and buried her face in his neck.

Finally, Ricky stood up and with a casual calmness said 'I'd better be going now'. Lynn nodded, beginning to cry, she could sense the tears behind his eyes although that crafty half smile of his was winning. Lynn, in reality, couldn't speak a word. She thoroughly said 'no', though with a shake of her head. However, she already knew that he was about to settle the matter in short shrift and watched as he backed the car out of the garage and onto the main road ... and was gone! He glanced back at her through the cracked driver's mirror, and glimpsed her little shape sitting cross-legged, head in hands, on the floor of the driveway. Ricky stopped the car abruptly, got out, and quickly walked back to where she was sitting: 'You wanna come too baby sister?' he frivolously asked. She nodded and simultaneously threw him a whopping smile!

Kiss Me Deadly

She could cry and make you feel ashamed and yet you'd burst with pride because she shared your name.

She is like a snowbird who so quickly flies and every time she looks at me, I celebrate her eyes.

Ricky Dale's

Forty-seven

Toronto is so darn hot in July! It has a harsh climate in any event. In winter it's often bitterly cold with sub-zero temperatures, but July and August are, on the other hand, uncomfortably hot and humid.

I had kept Edward G's home telephone number on a scrap of paper in my pocketbook. For some obscure reason he had told me to, and Edward G was not a man a person would question!

I called his number and, in two shakes of a lamb's tail, we had hailed a taxi and were heading out toward the Lawrence Avenue West neighbourhood. The links between Toronto and Italy are relatively solid in this are of the city. Edward G was sat leisurely on a careworn chaise longue on his neatly trimmed lawn, and got up to greet us. He invited us into his home and, not enquiring whether or not we wanted a drink, he went ahead and poured us both a somewhat large Cointreau with ice and lemon!

Ushering us to seats on his roofed veranda, he systematically began to connect us both with all the eventful stuff going down: 'As you know, Rocco was a highly respected boss in Southern Ontario for decades. When the contract was put out on you, we jumped through hoops to find you – even crossing the Atlantic on a couple of occasions. However, Rocco is dead now and the 'family' want no more involvement in pursuing your murder. They are of the opinion, as I myself am, that you are not to blame for the death of his Candelaria. You were, in fact, a gullible scapegoat that Rocco was able to hold responsible to save face.'

'What happened, why did he die?' I enquired.

'There was some bickering between the bosses. They had a big fall-out and his brother-in-law gunned him down at his home in Toronto. By all accounts, the last words that Rocco Zito uttered, as he pointed his firearm at his brother-in-law were: 'I will die, but you will die first!'

The brother-in-law lived to fight another day, notwithstanding being charged with first-degree murder! Sicilian newspapers have mentioned that 'constructive discussions have been going on, in order to get Rocco's killer released'.

At the end of the day, both Lynn and yours truly were uncertain whether or not to thank Edward G for his attentiveness and such. However, through past experience, I do know for sure that there definitely is a Cosa Nostra protocol. And not wanting to step outside their accepted code of behaviour, both Lynn and I shook his hand and thanked him profusely!

When we discussed matters at our hotel that evening, we were both absolutely of the opinion that, unless we'd taken the initiative in coming to Toronto now, we'd most probably be chasing our own tails and ducking in doorways for the rest of our lives!

Lynn made a 'funny' by adding: 'It's not usually the habit of Cosa Nostra to forward a letter of apology saying we've decided not to kill you after all!'

Having said all of that, we both agreed that Edward G really must have a soft spot – his farewell comments confirmed it: 'You kids go enjoy the rest of your lives, there are those in the "family" who have a high regard for the honourable way in which you both kept your unselfish allegiance to the "family" by not becoming a "rat"! I've mentioned this point to the bosses and we concur that, in the event that you wanna come back in, you are welcome to let us know!'

Puts me in mind of a line from Puzo's masterpiece, *The Godfather*:

"Keep your friends close but your enemies closer!"

Ivy geranium has sped across the front of the yard, strangling the dandelion and the rose alike. Flowering now in pink and white and almost red, it hides its tentacles. Still, you know that inch by inch underground and just above too, it slowly moves to capture this whole block. I doubt the hedge will offer much of a resistance. Three or so months should be enough to see it do its final battle. One last all-out offensive and every foot of ground will be geranium, made so in silence – no evidence of a proper plan. Indeed, so much is done in silence, and accomplished without a word!

The End

Addendum

Bugsy Siegel once remarked, inaccurately, that 'we only kill each other'. Mickey Cohen played the same refrain, insisting that 'I never killed nobody who didn't deserve it'. However, gangster Harry Pierpont may have said it best, addressing the prosecutor at his murder trial, he commented 'You'd probably be like me if you had the nerve'.

These modern day 'Robin Hoods' are reckless, outrageous and oftentimes bloody, but the one thing that they all have in common, their objective, is to aim high and not allow themselves to accept being second best.

I always knew that this was their common aim and didn't give a thought to upsetting the apple cart in any way, shape or form. Sure, I'd been 'supposedly' manipulated by law enforcement from time to time but they knew, my employers knew and I certainly knew that stonewalling was my best defence.

In any event, the 'Organisation' looked after me, and I was grateful to them! Perhaps that's the reason why, when the chips were down, they gave me the benefit of the doubt and allowed me some leeway –

at least Edward G did!

In hindsight, I wasn't treated as a loose end. Nevertheless, for several years the thought that I might have mistakenly forgotten to lock the door at night still put the fear of Christ into me. The fact that I'd seen many times exactly what they were capable of, never allowed me much respite at the time!

It seems to me that, in a sense, we need these so-called robber barons and their underground empires. In fact, in many respects, in the fabric of society that we have grown accustomed to living in, it's virtually impossible to tell a straight person from a crook!

From time to time, we've all had to seek 'direction' from our bank manager or perhaps our MP. It's worth bearing in mind that, although the customary handshake is acceptable, you may wish to top it up with a kiss – it's the ultimate sign of respect in Cosa Nostra language. It can also be interpreted as Cosa Nostra's sentence of death too. Dependent upon the nature of your 'meeting', you might want to choose!

About the Author

Ricky Dale is a former singer and lyric writer. Although recognised as a gifted wordsmith in his adopted Canada, when he finally returned to the UK, he was virtually unknown. His revival received a kickstart after he diversified by writing novels – this is his eighth. Ricky lives in a rambling maisonette on the coast, near the picturesque town of Torquay.

https://rickydaleauthor.wordpress.com

Kiss Me Deadly

Also by Ricky Dale

Limberlost
A semi-biographical account of famous soprano Krystyna Comanescu, a virtuoso who has fallen from favour and seeks to bring her austere demons to rest.

Limberlost II The Legacy
This book is the captivating sequel to *Limberlost*, in which secrets galore are let slip and the truth is exquisitely unearthed.

Limberlost III The Prequel
The prequel to *Limberlost*, and a most profoundly in-depth telling of not only how it all began, but the why and the who as well.

Cloudburst
An extremely personal insight into the fact-based account of why lovers Dahlia Carriera and Sandra Comanescu choose murder as a way of life.

I Knew The Bride When She Used To Rock 'n' Roll
A charming and emotional spooky tale, based on true happenings, which has been described as "Poltergeist meets The Sixth Sense".

Ricky Dale's

The House On Dundas And Vine
A beautifully haunting story about very powerful love between ordinary people doing extraordinary things in a quite ordinary way. Essentially a true story.

Siobhan's Bitches
A ménage à trois mini saga between infatuation and love … another virtually true story from the pen of Ricky Dale.

Kiss Me Deadly